January Hotwife

Hotwife of the Month Club 1

Lacey Cross

Copyright © 2024 by Lacey Cross

All rights reserved.

ISBN 13: 978-1-960162-16-8 (Paperback edition)

Cover design by Steph Brothers

No portion of this book may be reproduced in any form without written permission from the publisher or author, except as permitted by U.S. copyright law.

Contents

Chapter 1

My phone beeps with an incoming text message, and I swipe to read it just as I hear the front door open.

DEBRA

> I've got the craziest story to tell you. Call me ASAP.

Yeah...sorry, Debra. I've got a husband that I haven't seen in five days to kiss, so I don't have time to indulge in her drama. Debra's the wife of one of my husband's friends from college. I don't know her that well, but she likes to gossip. I'll text her later.

Henry calls out, "I'm home, baby."

I raise my voice and try to sound seductive as I stretch languidly on the couch. "In the living room."

My body's been buzzing with anticipation all day for Henry's return, and I could hardly focus on the book I was trying to kill time with. He told me he wanted me as soon as he got home, and I'm ready for him.

When he finally appears in the doorway, my heart skips a beat at the sight of him. He drops his bags and coat, and I stand up so I can run my hands over the sun-kissed skin of his arms. "Mmm, someone got some sun. You look so good after a trip," I whisper, pulling him closer for a kiss. "Did you have a pleasant flight?"

Every year, Henry joins his old college frat brothers on a trip to Aspen. I don't mind that the wives aren't invited; I'm not much of a skier, and the nights are just filled with poker and cigars for the men. It works out perfectly since I can plan my own girls' weekend getaways without any complaints from him—like the trip I'm taking next weekend. It's a win-win situation.

Henry sighs and hugs me. "Flight was fine, but traffic around the airport was a beast. I'm glad Will was driving and I got to relax. How've you been?"

Just being near him again warms my heart. "I missed you so much. I hate waking up without you so many days in a row."

Henry nuzzles my neck, and I shiver a little at the prickly stubble on his jawline.

"I'm so sorry I missed our morning ritual. I was thinking about you every day at seven in the morning. Every. Single. Morning." He punctuates his last three words with kisses along my neck, and it makes me giggle.

My husband loves to tease me right before he goes to work every day. He kisses me until I'm breathless and longing for more. Then he either plays with my nipples or rubs my pussy until I try to convince him to come back to bed...only to have him leave me panting as he goes to work. If he does his job well enough and gets me all hot and bothered, I run for a sex toy as soon as the front door clicks shut behind him.

I smile at him before shimmying my hips and rubbing against him. "You better not start anything you don't plan on finishing."

Henry groans and scoops me up in his arms, carrying me bridal-style up the stairs into our master suite. Ooooh, guess he's not going to get me worked up and leave me wet and needy tonight.

While Henry may not look like the guys you see on the covers of the romance novels I read, he knows exactly how to rock my world. He stays in shape and between his broad, muscular shoulders and deep brown eyes that make my insides melt, he's the perfect person for me. We just passed our ten-year anniversary, and we both feel lucky to have found each other.

Henry sets me on the floor of our bedroom, and we strip off each other's clothes, kissing as we reveal more and more skin. I'm down to just my bra and panties, but he's still got too many clothes on. I'm suddenly frantic to feel his naked skin against mine.

I struggle to get his shirt off, and he laughs as he helps me. "I think someone missed me."

"Less talk, more stripping."

I reach for the fly on his jeans, and he pushes my hand away. "Patience, my love."

Damn him. My entire body is tingling, and I just need his cock inside me. I step back from him a bit and unclasp my bra behind my back.

"You sure you want me to be patient?"

I slide my bra down my arms and let it drop on the floor before leaning forward to slip my panties off my ass. When they reach my ankles, I step out of them. What my husband doesn't know is that I had a spa appointment while he was gone and got a Brazilian bikini wax.

When I straighten up, his eyes drop to my smooth, bare mound, and the pupils in his eyes dilate with desire. I can see his erection jump in his jeans, and I try not to smile.

I climb up on the bed on my hands and knees with my ass facing him and look over my shoulder.

"So…" I purr at him and wiggle my ass. "Are you going to fuck me or not?"

Henry rips his pants off like a madman and climbs on the bed behind me. He grabs my hip with one hand, but as soon as I feel the tip of his cock pressing against my opening, he pauses.

"Baby?"

"Hmmm?" What game is my husband playing at now? My body trembles in anticipation, and I groan out, "Henry, don't tease me. I've been dying for your cock for days."

It's true. We usually have sex twice per week, fairly routine, so going five days without his cock isn't common.

He asks in a deep voice, "You're going to get what you want, but you have to answer a question for me first."

Henry gives my ass a quick spank and I let out a surprised squeak. It stings a little, but it only adds to the intense desire that's already coursing through me.

My voice drops an octave. "If you know what's good for you, you'll fuck me first, and then ask questions later."

He laughs and totally withdraws even the tip of his cock from me. "Someone doesn't want my cock that badly tonight."

"Fuck, Henry! You know how turned on I am. Put your cock inside me right now before I make you regret it."

My pussy aches with emptiness. I'm desperate to be filled by him, and when his cock brushes against my inner thigh, I mewl out in frustration. He's driving me crazy, and he knows it. I'm seconds away from begging for his cock, and he's enjoying drawing it out as long as possible. Damn my man and his excellent self-control.

With a finger, he draws a line from my clit, along my wet seam, and stops at the entrance of my pussy. He slides his digit inside me and slowly finger fucks me. My clit throbs and his tender touch sends sparks through my entire body. My head spins because it's not enough.

"So answer my question, and I'll fuck you as hard as you want." His voice is soft but commanding, and the authority it holds has my pussy contracting around his finger.

I'm desperate for release, but the delay is also driving me wild. I moan out, "Fine, what do you want to know so badly?"

He's still using his finger in slow, measured strokes, and I rock my hips back towards him.

He gives a throaty laugh. "Do you ever think of fucking someone other than me?"

My face flushes, and I'm suddenly glad I'm not looking at him. He's kidding, right? Why is he asking this?

I don't want to tell him that sometimes I imagine fucking some random hot guy I saw while I was out and about. It's never anyone he or I knows, so it's just a hot body without a real personality—it's fantasy.

Henry thrusts two fingers into me, but my thoughts are everywhere and I barely register it.

"Tell me and I'll give you my cock." His tone has lost its earlier playfulness.

I gasp out, "N...no."

Yes, yes, yes, a thousand times, yes. I want to scream out to my husband, but I keep it inside.

He stops moving his fingers and demands again, "Give me the truth, baby."

The raw lust in his voice shocks me to my very core. He wants me to have thought of fucking someone else. My mind spins, and I feel myself getting wetter. This is so fucking hot.

Something inside me cracks open, and I whimper out the truth, "Yes."

He moves his finger to my clit and rubs circles around it while holding his cock with the other hand and pressing against my opening, dipping the head just inside but pulling out again.

Henry croons, "Is your pussy soaked right now because you're thinking of fucking someone else?"

I wasn't thinking of anyone else until he said that, but suddenly I imagine there's a massive guy behind me—some biker-gang type with tattoos who looks like he'd make a woman sit in his lap all night being a cockwarmer while he chats with his friends.

I can't keep up with my husband, and my head whips around to look over my shoulder. His expression is smug when we lock gazes, and his fingers don't miss a beat as he continues to rub my clit.

"Come on baby, admit it."

He's pushing me farther than I ever thought he'd go, but I decide to go for broke and just blurt it out. "I imagine fucking other guys all the time. Happy?"

Henry plunges into me to the hilt, and I cry out in pleasure as he bottoms out.

"That's so sexy." Henry smacks my ass, and the stinging pain reverberates through my entire body.

Ohhhhh, god, he might be insane. I don't know what's gotten into him tonight. He's never this enthusiastic after a trip, but I'm loving it.

He fucks me in a punishing rhythm. Each stroke knocks me forward while I moan in ecstasy. The pleasure builds in layers, and I'm not going to be able to stop myself from coming. I briefly imagine he's the biker guy fucking me, but everything about what's happening is familiar, so the fantasy is short-lived. I don't really want to fuck someone else; I just want my husband.

When he spanks my ass again and picks up speed, I explode with an orgasm, crying out with pleasure. My entire body shakes as waves of bliss ripple from my core, and my climax triggers his. His cock spasms deep in my pussy as he bathes my walls in thick ribbons of his warm cum. I swear I can feel every spurt.

I'm still on my hands and knees, and I give a soft grunt when he pulls out and falls onto the bed next to me on his back.

When he holds out an arm, I settle against his side and rest my head on his shoulder with one hand on his chest and a leg thrown across his.

My brain is a jumbled mess as I whisper out, "What was that all about?"

Henry chuckles and wraps his free arm around my shoulder, holding me tightly against his chest. "The guys were talking in Aspen. One of the guys' wives fucks other men with his permission."

Huh. I trace patterns in his smattering of chest hair and say nothing. It's a pleasant fantasy.

Henry squeezes me and nuzzles his nose into my hair, breathing deeply. "I liked the idea more than I thought I would. If you ever want to try it, I'm game."

A small flutter of pleasure zaps my clit, but I don't want to sound enthusiastic about the idea, because I don't think I'd ever do it. "After tonight, who needs other men?"

He kisses my forehead. "Well, just know if you ever want to, you have my blessing as long as you tell me before and afterwards—like on your trip next week."

I laugh lightly. "Uh-huh, okay. I'll fuck my way through the entire resort over the week."

A low rumble comes through his chest. "Why don't you just start with one guy, and we see how it goes, okay?"

An erotic thrill flares through me at the idea of having sex with another man with Henry's approval. I never thought this was even an option, and I need time to think about it.

"Okay, honey." I snuggle against him and we both relax, lost in our thoughts.

Chapter 2

Felicity, my best friend in the entire world, pokes me from the lounge chair next to me. "January, did you notice how many hot guys are at this resort?"

It's shortly after lunchtime on the second day of my girls' trip, and Felicity and I came down to the pool to sunbathe. I crack my eyes open to look at her, and she tips her head to gesture across the pool deck. A smile curves up the sides of my lips as I spot three men hanging around the poolside bar. All three men look delicious.

When one tall, blonde-haired guy in blue swim trunks turns around with his drink, I suck in a sharp breath. Yummy. His face is classically handsome, with sculpted cheekbones and perfectly trimmed facial hair around his jawline and chin. He's fit with an incredible build—in fact, he's massive. He towers over the other guys, and my pussy hums to life.

My mouth is practically watering, and I have a sudden urge to fuck this man even though he's definitely the biggest man I've ever looked at in the flesh. If his cock is as big as the rest of him, that's one challenge I'd love to accept.

The giant turns back to his friends, and my gaze flickers to Felicity. I try to make a joke to hide how hot and bothered I suddenly am. "Yep, we're in heaven. Can it get any better than this?"

We're at a posh retreat on a private island for a long week-end. It's an exclusive getaway that caters to adults twenty-one and older. It's the ultimate paradise, with activities, a beach, bars, a hot tub, a pool, and, of course, a spa. We had massages and mani/pedis yesterday, and tonight is a huge bonfire down on the beach.

"Oooh, speaking of hot, check out those two." Felicity raises her sunglasses to peek at a couple of guys walking by and gives them an approving nod.

Those guys are attractive, but they can't hold a candle to the massive blonde guy. Felicity says something, but my mind wanders as I watch the hot blondie with his friends out of the corner of my eye. If given the chance, would I fuck him? Nah, I wouldn't go through with it. The fantasy is fun, but I'm not really that kind of woman.

I'm suddenly thirsty, and I take a sip from my bottle of water to quench my dry throat as Felicity catches my eye and says, "Did you hear Marilyn fucks other guys and James lets her?"

I sputter, and liquid goes down the wrong pipe and I have a coughing fit. Felicity looks worried for a minute before my fit dies down. The giant must have overheard me choking because when I sneak a glance over in his direction, he's looking directly at me with a concerned expression. I flash him a quick smile and then glare over at my friend.

"Are you trying to kill me?" I hiss out as quietly as I can so I don't attract any more attention.

My bestie just grins. "Debra's got her panties all in a wad over it, but if my husband would let me, I'd take a guy in each hole and thank them afterwards."

I'm glad I'm not taking another drink. Just imagining her husband, Edward, wanting to share her is pretty hilarious. He's the stuffiest dude I've ever met. How he scored a hot-blooded, sexy wife like Felicity, I'll never know, but she seems happy.

I guess I also now know what Debra wanted to talk about last week. I kept forgetting to text her back. Hopefully she'll forgive me when I message her after the trip.

I swing my legs off the lounger and face her. "I need to go back to the room. I've got to call Henry and take a nap before dinner and the bonfire. You coming with?"

"Nah." She shakes her head and stares off towards the group of men by the bar. "You head up, I'm going to enjoy the eye candy some more."

"Okay then, see you at dinner." I grab my bag before heading up to my room. I don't like to share rooms when I go on these vacations, because I want to have private conversations with my husband easily and I sleep better when there isn't someone else with me. It works out fine since Felicity enjoys her privacy as well.

In my room, I'm a bundle of excitement for no real reason. My hands shake as I hold the phone and dial my husband to video chat with him. He's got poker tonight, so hopefully I catch him before he leaves.

When Henry answers the call, he's shirtless, which makes my mouth water. They say distance makes the heart grow fonder, but next year I don't think I'm going to schedule a trip so soon after he gets back from Aspen. I needed at least another week of sex before being separated from him again.

Henry flashes me a charming grin. "You have good timing. I'm changing and heading out for poker. How's my wonderful wife today?"

The sight of his smile tugs at my heart, and my voice comes out a little husky. "Your girl's horny and wishing you were here."

My husband sits down on the edge of the bed and winks at me. "I bet there are plenty of guys around to help with that. Remember what I said."

As if I could forget. "They aren't you."

He chuckles and stretches his arms out wide, flexing his biceps, before dropping his hands. "Come on, tell me, did someone catch your eye?"

I bite my bottom lip and consider telling him the truth about the enormous guy at the pool.

"Wait." Henry sets the phone down on the bed before I say anything. A moment later he picks it up and aims it at his naked and erect dick. "Now tell me."

He holds the phone camera directed at his cock and slowly starts stroking his length with his other hand. Holy shit. Watching his shaft turn shiny from pre-cum has me so wet I can feel my bikini bottoms sticking to me.

"Show me your pussy, January."

My core pulses and my stomach clenches with desire as I untie the strings of my bikini bottom and spread my legs, pointing the camera so he can see between them.

My pussy lips are glistening, and when I run a finger down my slit, I moan and lift my hips off the bed to meet my fingers. I roll my clit under the pads of my index and middle finger. It feels so good that I know I could come quickly, but I also like the torture.

Henry groans. "Baby, I've got to go. I'm picking up dinner on the way. But promise me something."

"Anything," I breathe out as my fingers continue working their magic on my swollen clit.

"If you meet a guy you like, you have my full blessing to do whatever you want, okay? Promise me you won't hold back out of concern for me."

The muscles deep in my abdomen seize, and my orgasm teeters on a razor's edge. I barely manage to whisper, "Yes, honey."

My husband blows a kiss and then ends the call.

I remove my hand from between my legs and slump back on the bed, shivering from how close I was to coming. When the image of the blonde-haired guy pops back into my head and I picture him above me on the bed, fucking me, I almost start rubbing my clit again. Will I see him tonight, and could I get him alone?

Oh god, am I nuts? I'm starting to actually consider fucking someone else.

Crawling up to the pillow, I settle in and close my eyes. I'll get my nap, and I'm sure the feeling will disappear once I'm no longer horny.

CHAPTER 3

There are more people at the bonfire than I expected, and the laughter is infectious as it swirls around me. This party is such a different vibe when it's all adults on vacation. It almost seems like a college party.

The beach is dark, but it's a warm night, so I'm just wearing a sundress and sandals. I put my long blonde hair up in a ponytail, and I know I look sexy. I tried to tell myself it wasn't for the blonde guy the entire time I was getting ready, but it was.

I came down here with Felicity, but we quickly separated to get drinks and flirt with other guys. You'd think we weren't two married women, but I'm not going to judge her, since my husband actually wants me to fuck someone. That's way beyond flirting.

I see the massive blonde guy several times and we keep catching each other's eyes. Every time our gaze connects, a tingle of awareness runs through my body. There's always an appreciative look on his face, and knowing he finds me attractive makes me even more turned on than I was earlier when I was daydreaming about fucking him.

Shit, I need a drink. He's going to keep me thirsty all night at this rate. Since I want a clear head, I grab a soda instead of anything alcoholic and wander off the main beach area to walk the shore. The sand is wet and firm beneath my sandals, and the foamy crest of each wave that hits the shore flows over my toes before receding back into the ocean.

I close my eyes and tilt my head back, soaking up the gentle breeze washing over me. A moment later, I hear a man clearing his throat. I whip my head toward the noise and see the giant standing a short distance away, looking at me. I'm not surprised it's him.

Since he has a can of soda in his hand, he gestures with his head towards the path. "May I walk with you?"

This is it, the opportunity my husband is encouraging me to take advantage of. The strange thrill from earlier comes rushing back, and I hope my voice doesn't sound breathy when I say, "I'd like that."

His face lights up with a smile, and the brightness of it fills me with a mixture of nervousness and excitement.

He offers his hand to me. "I'm Adam."

I give him my customary greeting that I've perfected over the years whenever I meet someone new. "I'm January—like the month. It's nice to meet you."

I slip my hand into his massive one. His grip is firm as we shake, and my brain short circuits. The masculine strength that emanates from him sends shivers to my core, and a delicious ache of longing for him builds inside me.

He drops my hand and we fall in step with one another. Neither one of us speaks as we make our way further down the beach. I glance at him out of the corner of my eye, and his broad shoulders seem to brush the stars. Besides being impressively sized, the top of my head barely reaches mid-chest on him. I'm not a tall woman, but he'd tower over almost anyone. Hell, how would I even fuck this guy? I imagine riding him, and the mechanics of that send a tingling spark through my pussy and I have to shift to ease the ache.

"So, have you ever been here before?" Adam finally breaks the silence.

I startle out of my mental daydream of riding him. "Um, yeah, every few years I come with my friends. You?"

He shakes his head. "First time here for me."

We're getting close to the end of the beach section for the resort, and we angle towards one of the wooden docks on the outskirts where boats come to deliver goods and take guests to and from the island. I never come down to these docks other than when I first arrive at the resort or when I leave. I've never had a reason.

As we walk, the beach becomes darker around us. The sounds of laughter from the bonfire fade into the distance. We are surrounded by the ocean on one side and sand dunes on the other, with the dock looming ahead. In just a few steps, we will have to turn back.

I don't want to go back. I'm here with him, and I have a choice to make. Stopping in my tracks, he pauses also with a curious look on his face.

The moonlight reflects in his eyes, and he gives me an encouraging smile. "So, what made you want to come for a walk with me? Not that I mind the company."

My pulse flutters as I swallow and lick my suddenly parched lips. "My husband said I could have sex with someone on this trip. He gave me his blessing."

Adam chuckles, a mischievous glint in his eyes. His gaze is intense, and I can't remember why I didn't want to fuck someone else when he says, "Well then, that changes things."

What does it change? Before I can gather the courage to ask, Adam steps closer to me and tilts my chin up with a gentle touch. "But do you want what your husband wants?"

I hesitate for a moment, my mind filled with doubts. But then I remember how turned on I've been thinking about fucking him, and how Henry is encouraging it. This is my chance to do something wild and crazy, and I'm going to take it.

I take a deep breath and confess. "Yes."

My stomach lurches like I'm falling and when Adam slides his arm around my waist, it's only his grip on me that keeps me stable. "Have you been thinking of fucking me?"

I'm tongue-tied as his closeness and the warmth of him fries my brain. He must read the answer from my face.

Adam brings his lips down to my neck, brushing lightly against my skin, and it's so tantalizing that I sway towards him.

His voice is a dark whisper. "What do you want me to do to you?"

I can feel his cock harden through his pants, and I press closer against him. The size of him both thrills and intimidates me. A shudder runs through me, and I gasp out, "Make me scream so loud that if anyone walks past, they'd hear."

He shifts and pushes me closer to the dock until my back runs into one of the wooden support beams. He takes my soda can from my hand and sets both of our cans on the edge of the dock before lifting me off the ground effortlessly. I wrap my legs around him as a pleasurable tingle zips through me. Holy shit, he's holding me like I weigh nothing.

"Lean back and grip the edge," he says in a husky voice as he tugs my dress up to my breasts, exposing my panties and stomach.

My hands scramble to find purchase on the wood. It takes me a second, but I finally grip it while leaning my back against the dock. The air is cool on my exposed skin but feels refreshing with the contrast of the heat radiating off him. I'm a trembling, aching ball of need, but I force myself to maintain eye contact with him.

Adam drags my underwear to the side before reaching for his zipper. He frees his cock from his pants, and I look down to see how big he is. Wow. That is one hell of a cock. My inner muscles clench with hunger as I eye his length. I suddenly feel powerful and sexy in a way that I haven't felt in a long time. I know my husband loves and desires me, but to have this effect on a guy I just met is a heady experience.

His dick is impressive. Long with a broad crown. The ridge around his cockhead is thick, and my stomach clenches with anticipation. I'm wet and needy, and he hasn't done more than just show me his cock. My senses are overwhelmed with anticipation, and a shiver runs through me. Yeah, it doesn't matter. I want him. My nipples strain against my dress, needing attention, and every inch of me aches.

Adam growls out a demand. "Ask me to fuck you."

I love how commanding he's being, and I feel a jolt of desire. My heart hammers as I whimper, "Please fuck me."

"Ask again and use my name."

My pulse quickens even more. I need him in me, and the tip of his cock brushes against my center, taunting me with how close he is to me. He's so hard, but the softness of the velvety smooth skin drives me crazy with lust.

I arch my hips closer to his and grind against him, trying to find some friction for my aching clit. "Please fuck me, Adam."

He holds me stable with one hand while he pushes my dress and bra up over my tits, exposing them to the night air. Imagining what I'd look like if someone saw us from the beach has my blood boiling in my veins, and I tremble in his grasp, nearly frantic to get his cock inside me.

He pinches and pulls on my nipples roughly before releasing them. The sting is slightly painful and turns me on even more. If he doesn't fuck me soon, he's going to have a crazed woman in his hands.

"Keep your eyes on me while I fuck you, and say my name when you come," he demands in a tone that leaves no argument.

"Yes," I mewl out and try to tighten my thighs around him to get him to shove his cock inside me. He's clearly got something about me using his name, and it's hot. I'll scream his name out if he gives me an amazing orgasm.

Adam aligns himself at my opening and slowly starts to push in, giving me every inch in slow, steady movements. Holy fuck, he's thicker than I realized. Once he's in as deep as he can go, I can't hold in my cry of ecstasy. This feels incredible.

"God, you're tight." Adam grits out the words while he pauses for a minute to allow me to adjust to him—if I even can adjust to him. His cock is stretching me out farther than I've ever been before.

I lock my eyes on his and feel every twitch of his shaft buried deep within me. He starts to pull out, and it feels like my core tries to cling to him on purpose to prevent him from withdrawing. Oh fuck, this feels so good, I'm going to be thinking about his cock in the future. I'm not sure my husband realizes what he's unleashed inside me.

Once he pulls back until just his cockhead remains lodged within me, he pushes forward with one fluid movement, and I cry out in pleasure. Every nerve ending is alive, and for one moment it's like I'm hovering above my body, staring down at how raunchy it is to fuck a guy I don't know on the beach. As he fucks me, I return to my body, mentally let go of all the "what-ifs and doubts," and embrace my sluttiest side. I'm ravenous for his cock, and I need him to fuck me hard.

He sets a grueling pace, and my moans reach higher in pitch as I keep up with his thrusts. My hands lose their grip on the pier, and I wrap them around his neck instead as he fucks me into a frenzy. Each time he spears into me, the base of his cock rubs my clit and sends sparks up my spine. The stimulation is maddening, and I'm desperate for whatever is going to make me come. I try to bounce against him and fuck him like he's a standing sex toy. His cock is so fucking amazing I could impale myself on it every day and climax.

Oh yeah, I'm such a slut and my husband is the most amazing man in the world for letting me do this.

He bends his head forward and captures one of my nipples with his lips, sucking hard until it reaches the threshold between pleasure and pain. His words rumble out of him against my breast. "You fucking love this, don't you?"

A tremor passes through my body at the sheer need in his voice, and I pant out a response. "Yes, I love being a slut."

Adam bites my nipple in retribution for my brazen comment and then lifts his head and focuses on his thrusts. The pleasure builds deep in my core, and I'm crying out every time he hits a magical spot deep inside me.

I throw my head back and squeeze my eyes shut while every muscle in my body begins to tense, ready to explode. The pressure builds, and when my eyes snap open again, the passion in his gaze locks on to mine. I can tell by the harsh tone of his breathing and the deep flush spreading on his cheeks that he's as affected as I am by what we're doing. We are like two animals mating on a public beach without shame.

This isn't me—or it wasn't. This is not who I thought I was when I came on this trip. Yet I've embraced it, and I wouldn't stop it for anything. The physical connection is too addictive—he's too addictive. Everything about him sets me on fire.

When he thrusts harder, I see stars, and my muscles clamp down on his cock when the tension finally breaks.

"Ooooh, god!" I scream as I come undone.

My nails dig into his shoulders as my walls pulse and squeeze him as the orgasm rips through me. I cry out his name in a rising crescendo as all my senses explode in bliss.

He fucks me through my orgasm, prolonging the pleasure, and just when I think he's going to come with me, he unhooks my legs from around him and sets my feet on the sand.

What's going on? My brain is too fuzzy to understand anything while he leans over and brushes his lips against mine before pulling me against him. His kiss is full of passion and lust, and I savor the taste of him. My arms creep around his shoulders as my head spins. I don't care what happens next.

He rips his mouth from mine and orders, "Turn around and bend over."

I can't think beyond obeying him, so I turn and place my hands on the wooden beam, dipping low until my ass is in the air. I gasp when he tears my panties off with a sharp jerk and tosses them aside before stepping close and kicking my feet wider apart. Wetness drips down my thighs, and I'm curious if he can see it.

When he drops to his knees, I'm surprised and then almost giggle. Yeah, I bet he can see exactly how wet I am.

When he traces his fingers along the seam of my pussy, he groans. My pussy aches to be filled again, and I push backwards, trying to tempt him to fuck me again.

He toys with my opening for a moment, swirling a finger in circles around my slick heat before plunging two digits deep in me. I moan and rock against his hand, loving how his fingers feel as he pumps them in and out of me. My knees threaten to buckle, but he stills behind me.

"Promise me you'll tell your husband every detail about tonight and let him know how much you enjoyed fucking me."

The demand in his voice surprises me, and a thrill runs down my spine. I don't have a problem sharing the details of tonight with my husband, since that was our agreement.

"I will," I promise.

He stops fingering my pussy. "Stand up and turn around."

When I do what he says, he shifts his position in the sand to stretch his legs out in front of him and reaches for my hand, tugging me down, facing him. I straddle him, and the sand cushions my knees. Yeah, we're going to be a mess when we're done.

My dress is still pushed up above my tits, and my bra is holding the fabric up. Adam plays with my nipples as I position his cock so I can rub up and down the length without him being inside me.

Adam's breathing increases, and he grits out in a gravelly voice, "Fuck yourself on me and make me come."

His dirty command has my pussy contracting in anticipation as more wetness slips out and coats his shaft. I consider teasing him some more, but I want his cock back inside me too much to wait.

I lower myself onto his shaft while he rolls both of my nipples between his fingers. Pleasure heads straight to my clit, and I cry out as he fills me again. After his entire length is seated inside me, it's like a switch is flipped on in my brain and I go wild.

I ride him, rolling my hips, and he moves his hands down my body to put one on my hip while the other dives between my legs. He caresses my clit, flicking the swollen nub as I try to drive him deeper and harder inside me. I lean back, putting my hands on the sand so I can change the angle of his cock as it moves in and out. I slam against him to the hilt repeatedly as he continues to brush circles around my clit with his finger.

Nothing matters but the pleasure. I'm moaning continuously as I hurtle towards another orgasm, lost to the rapture.

When he rubs my clit faster, I detonate into bliss with a drawn-out mewl that transforms into an "Oh, Adam!" as my entire body shakes and shivers. White-hot pleasure cascades through me.

He bucks into me as I ride the orgasm out while circling my hips, rocking my pussy against him while my inner walls contract again. A hard thrust from him, and fireworks go off in my head. I come a third time as I cry out loudly and my entire body quivers.

His cock pulses inside me, and his own groans of ecstasy reverberate in the air as I collapse forward and his warm cum floods my inner depths. His thigh muscles quiver as he finishes unloading, and I kiss him softly as he comes down from his orgasm.

When I can tell he's done, I slump onto his chest while my brain blanks out for a few moments.

Holy shit, I just fucked someone on the beach where any-one could have seen us.

After a few minutes, he stirs beneath me and helps me pull my bra and dress down. I'm giggling as I stand up and he joins me and adjusts his clothes and picks up my panties, pocketing them. Yeah, he can toss them. I'm going to walk back to the hotel with his cum dripping down my inner thighs to feel like the ultimate slut.

When our clothes are straightened, he pulls me against him for a hug. "Was that good for you?"

I laugh. "As if you couldn't tell. That was amazing."

"Yes, it was." His voice is deep with appreciation, and I know he means it.

We kiss tenderly for a minute until it threatens to get hot and heavy. I don't want Felicity to worry, so I step back from him. He grabs our soda cans, and I hook my arm through his as we head back up the beach.

When we get close to the bonfire, we pause and I look at him. "Thank you for a fun evening."

He winks at me. "No, thank you. Have a wonderful rest of your trip."

We split up as we get to the group of people. Felicity finds me shortly afterwards and gives me a long, questioning look. I'm sure I look like I was just fucked. She opens her mouth to say something, and I put my finger to my lips. "Not now. Let's talk tomorrow."

She nods, and I go to find another soda. I need something to drink after that workout. For the next hour, I can feel Felicity's eyes on me, and I have to stop myself from giggling. She's going to be shocked when she finds out what I did, but my husband deserves to be the first one who hears it.

CHAPTER 4

I told my husband everything that happened before bed that night and then Felicity the next day. She took it better than I expected and kept calling me a slut in an admiring way, but my husband's response was all that really mattered to me. When I told him, he got quiet and said to expect to be fucked hard when I got home.

And now I'm home.

My entire body is humming with desire as I walk in the front door.

"Hello, baby." Henry steps into the hallway as I set down my luggage, and my heart skips a beat. He was clearly waiting for me.

I rush over to him and fling my arms around him, inhaling deeply as his scent floods my senses, a mix of warm skin, musky cologne, and the familiar scent of our laundry detergent. God, I missed him.

When he nuzzles my neck, a shiver runs through me, and my nerves dance with electricity as I look at my husband and giggle. "So what now?"

His voice is a sensual whisper near my ear and his breath tickles me when he replies, "I want to hear all of it again—every naughty thought or deed—leave nothing out."

My husband wraps his arm around me and leads me to the bedroom. I don't have time to take off my clothes before he pushes me on my back and peels off my pants and panties.

I sit up on my elbows and stare at Henry. "I can't believe I'm turned on by the thought of telling you what I did with another man."

"I'm excited too. Now start talking." His voice is hoarse, and I hear his belt buckle clink before it drops on the floor.

I stare up at Henry. He's more handsome than he's ever been, and he's looking at me like he owns me, like I belong to him, and I do. A deep craving twists in my stomach, and my body calls out for him.

Henry pulls his jeans off, and his cock bounces out. God, I need him inside me. I spread my legs as he climbs up on the bed and crawls to me, pushing my shirt up so that he can capture a nipple in his mouth. I cry out when his cock slides inside of me.

The look on Henry's face is primal. "You like getting your pussy filled with cock?"

"Only yours," I sigh as he bottoms out.

He smirks. "Liar. Now talk."

It's hard to form words as he starts fucking me vigorously. "It started when I saw a sexy guy at the pool..."

I pause when Henry slams his hips into me, but I love this side of my husband. So while he fucks me, the entire story tumbles out. Every thrust and groan from him tells me he loves my slutty side.

Henry fucks me in a steady rhythm as my climax builds. Right before I orgasm, I whisper the last bit to my husband. "I liked getting fucked by someone else, but you're the one I love and nothing will change that."

Henry kisses me passionately, swallowing my moans as he gives a deep, possessive thrust that tips me over the edge, and I climax while clinging to him. The pleasure washes over me, and I moan loudly while he groans that he's coming. The pleasure swells and spreads as Henry gives a shuddering thrust and bathes my inner walls with his cum. His release triggers a series of mini spikes of bliss, and I writhe beneath him.

My husband is the perfect man for me, and he holds me in his arms as my mind clears. All I want is him. No one else matters.

After we come down from our high, I curl up into a ball next to Henry with a contented sigh and run my fingers through the hair on his chest. "So I guess I'm now officially a hotwife."

My husband laughs and wraps an arm around me, pulling me tight to his side. "You mean you're *my* hotwife, and I *might* agree to share you again if you beg good enough."

My core hums to life again with the promise of more adventures to come. When the time is right, I'm going to beg like he's never seen me beg before.

The End

ABOUT LACEY CROSS

Lacey Cross is a wife sharing erotica writer with over 100 short stories published since she started in 2021. Her stories emphasize the pleasure found from the wife living her best slut life and embracing the hotwife lifestyle. She explores themes of free use, submissive wives with dominant bulls, BDSM... and oh-so-many men.

Find her books, erotic shorts, and audiobooks on her website:
https://lacey-cross.com/

If you like romantic erotica BDSM, check out April Cross's books at:
https://books.april-cross.com/

www.ingramcontent.com/pod-product-compliance
Lightning Source LLC
Chambersburg PA
CBHW030013010826
48973CB00009B/2783